This Walker Book belongs to:

....

For Dillon and Wilf, with love.

First published 2026 by Walker Books Ltd
87 Vauxhall Walk, London SE11 5HJ

2 4 6 8 10 9 7 5 3 1

EU Authorized Representative: HackettFlynn Ltd, 36 Cloch Choirneal, Balrothery, Co. Dublin, K32 C942, Ireland
EU@walkerpublishinggroup.com

This work has been typeset in Minion Pro

Printed in China

British Library Cataloguing in Publication Data: a catalogue record for this book is available from the British Library.

ISBN 978-1-5295-3317-0 (hb)
ISBN 978-1-5295-2384-3 (pb)

www.walker.co.uk

WALKER BOOKS
AND SUBSIDIARIES
LONDON • BOSTON • SYDNEY • AUCKLAND

THE GOOD DEED DOGS

Emma Chichester Clark

Bodger, Billy and Betty were very good dogs.
They liked to do good deeds.

They really liked helping people and were
always looking out for ways to be useful.

One morning, Bodger, Billy and Betty noticed an old lady who was carrying some heavy shopping.
"Quick!" said Bodger. "Let's do a good deed."

"We're here to help," said Billy and Betty.
"Leave it to us!" said Bodger.
"Help!" cried the old lady.
"Help! Help!"

She gripped her bags tightly, but the helpers kept on helping. And the little old lady still didn't let go …
and then …

CALAMITY!

The bags ripped,
vegetables flew, fruit
smashed and everything
went everywhere.

Bodger's, Billy's and Betty's hearts sank. Their ears drooped.

"We're SO sorry," said Bodger.
"We were trying do a good deed," said Billy and Betty.
"Well, if you want to do a good deed, you can clear up all this mess," said the old lady.

So, they did.

Later that day, the little helpers noticed a man watering some hanging baskets. “Quick!” said Bodger, “let’s do a good deed.”

“We’re here to help,” said Billy and Betty. “Leave it to us!” said Bodger.

But the ladder was
wobbly and the man
started shouting.
"Help!" he cried,
waving his arms.

But the helpers went on helping.
"Help! Help!" the man cried as he swayed
back and forth … and then …

CALAMITY!

He tumbled with a crash.
Everything went everywhere.

Bodger's, Billy's and Betty's
hearts sank. Their
ears drooped.

"We're SO sorry," said Bodger.
"We were trying to do a good
deed," said Billy and Betty.
"Well, if you want to do a good
deed, you can clear up all this
mess," said the man.

So, they did.

In the afternoon, the little helpers were looking out for someone to help when they saw a girl hanging out her washing. It was very windy.

"Quick!" said Bodger.
"Let's do a good deed."
"We're here to help!"
cried Billy and Betty.
"Leave it to us!" said Bodger.
But the wind was strong
and terribly gusty.

"Oh! Help!" cried the girl, as a
tablecloth flew. And the
helpers went on helping.
Sheets were swirling,
pillowcases billowing,
socks soaring …

and then …

CALAMITY!

Everything went everywhere
and all the knickers and vests
were caught in the trees.

Bodger's, Billy's and Betty's hearts sank. Their ears drooped.

"We're SO sorry," said Bodger.
"We just wanted to do a good deed," said Billy and Betty.
"Well, if you want to do a good deed, you can get all my washing and put it back where it belongs!" said the girl.

So, they did.

After that, Bodger, Billy and Betty,
their ears drooping, walked sadly home.
"Maybe we're no good at doing good deeds," said Bodger.
"Nobody really wants us to help them," said Billy.
"Maybe we'd better give up," sighed Betty.

SUDDENLY ...

a loud scream made all
their ears stand up on end.

"HELP! HELP!"

A little girl was crying and pointing at the river. Bobbing along in the water was a large saucepan with a tiny kitten inside it. There wasn't a moment to lose.

The three little helpers dived in.
They hit the water with a gigantic

SPLASH,

and then …

The saucepan bounced
up … up … up …

and the kitten soared
up … up … up …

and then down …

and landed safely in
the little girl's arms.

Everyone came to see, and everyone was delighted. Bodger, Billy and Betty shook themselves dry.

“Thank you,” said the girl’s father.
“That was a very, very good deed.”

"Happy to help!" said Bodger.
"Our pleasure," said Billy and Betty.

"Well, in that case, perhaps you'd like to come and help us with some odd jobs around the house?" said the girl's father.

So,
they did.